Hannah's Baby Sister

BY MARISABINA RUSSO

Greenwillow Books, New York

Gouache paints were used to prepare the full-color art.
The text type is Futura Medium BT.

Printed in Hong Kong by South China Printing Company (1988) Ltd.
First Edition   10 9   8   7   6   5   4   3   2   1

Library of Congress Cataloging-in-Publication Data
Russo, Marisabina.
Hannah's baby sister / by Marisabina Russo.
p.   cm.
Summary: Hannah, who is sure that the new baby in her family
is going to be a girl, eagerly looks forward to having a little sister.
ISBN 0-688-15831-5 (trade).   ISBN 0-688-15832-3 (lib. bdg.)
[1. Babies—Fiction.   2. Brothers and sisters—Fiction.
I. Title.   PZ7.R9192Han   1998   [E]—dc21
97-31412   CIP   AC

For
Patti Chenis

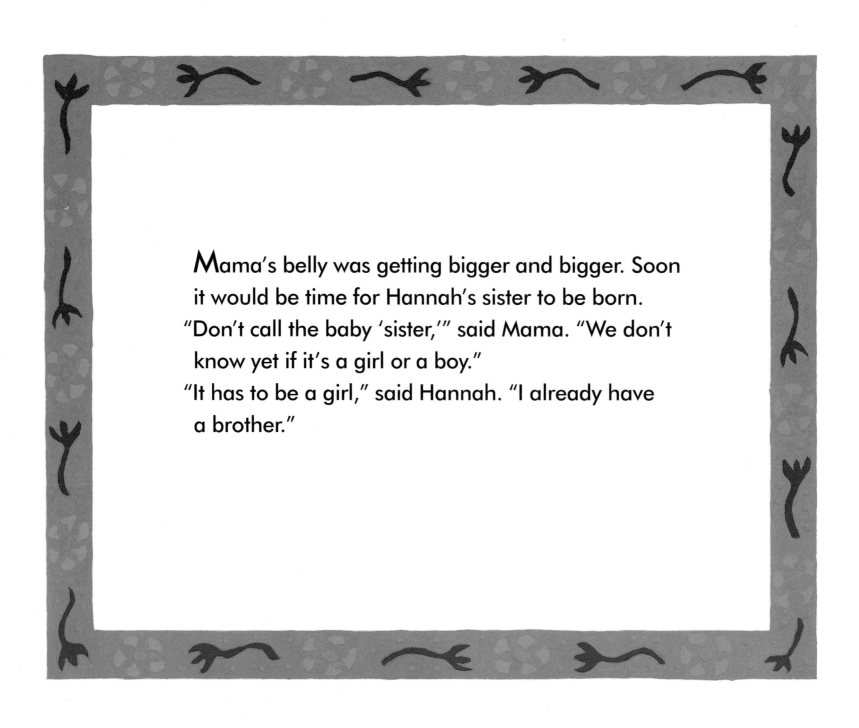

Mama's belly was getting bigger and bigger. Soon it would be time for Hannah's sister to be born.

"Don't call the baby 'sister,'" said Mama. "We don't know yet if it's a girl or a boy."

"It has to be a girl," said Hannah. "I already have a brother."

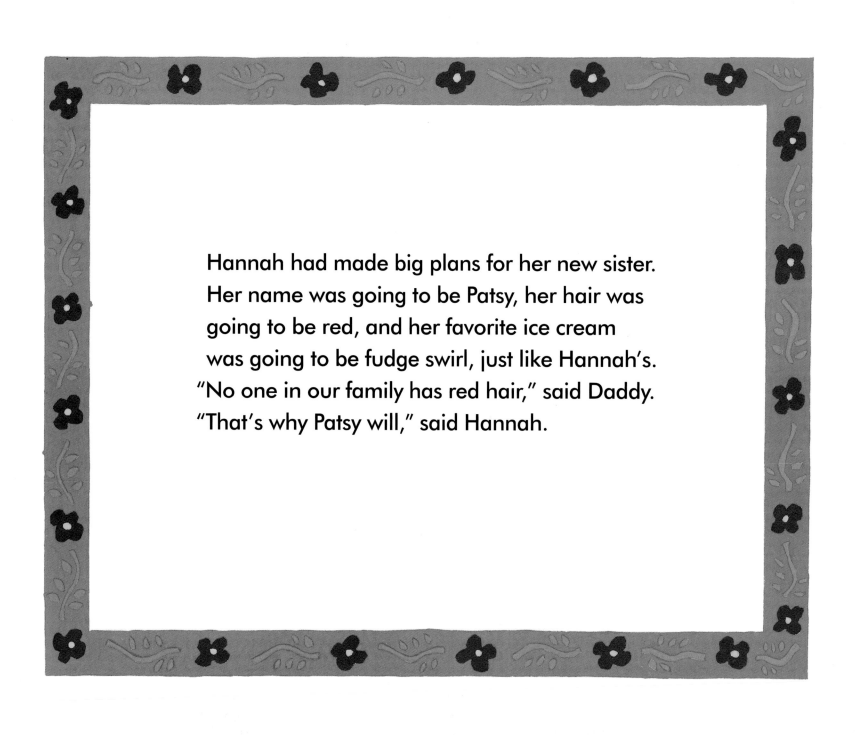

Hannah had made big plans for her new sister.
Her name was going to be Patsy, her hair was
going to be red, and her favorite ice cream
was going to be fudge swirl, just like Hannah's.
"No one in our family has red hair," said Daddy.
"That's why Patsy will," said Hannah.

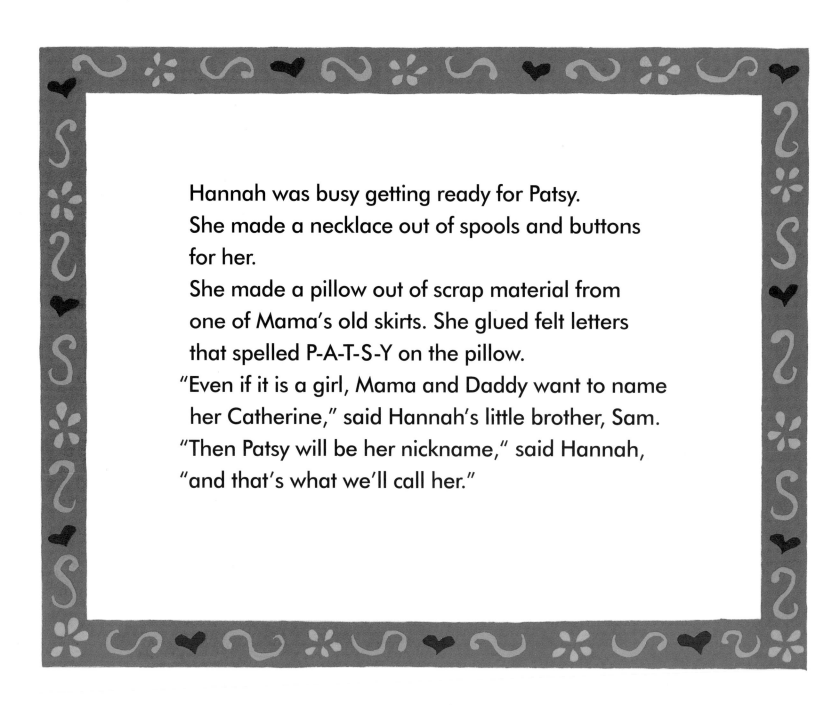

Hannah was busy getting ready for Patsy.
She made a necklace out of spools and buttons
for her.
She made a pillow out of scrap material from
one of Mama's old skirts. She glued felt letters
that spelled P-A-T-S-Y on the pillow.
"Even if it is a girl, Mama and Daddy want to name
her Catherine," said Hannah's little brother, Sam.
"Then Patsy will be her nickname," said Hannah,
"and that's what we'll call her."

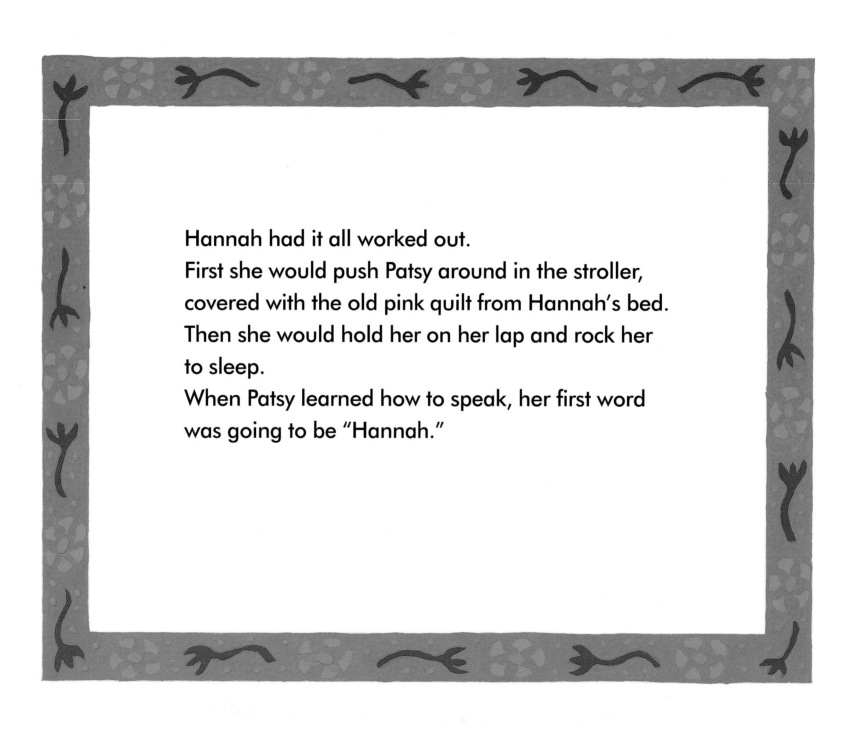

Hannah had it all worked out.
First she would push Patsy around in the stroller,
covered with the old pink quilt from Hannah's bed.
Then she would hold her on her lap and rock her
to sleep.
When Patsy learned how to speak, her first word
was going to be "Hannah."

When it was almost time for the new baby to be born, Hannah's grandma came to stay with them. Grandma loved to play the piano. Every morning and every evening Grandma played songs and Hannah sang along. Hannah changed the words so she could sing about Patsy.

One morning when Hannah woke up, Mama and Daddy were not home. Grandma was in the kitchen cooking oatmeal.

"Mama felt the baby coming," said Grandma. "She and Daddy went to the hospital an hour ago."

Hannah, Grandma, and Sam ate some oatmeal. Hannah kept waiting for the phone to ring.

"What's taking them so long?" she said.

"Babies are born when they're good and ready," said Grandma.

Hannah made a "welcome home" sign with markers.
It said, "Welcome to the best little sister in the whole
world."
"Maybe you ought to make another sign to welcome
a little brother, just in case," said Grandma.
"NO!" said Hannah.

Hannah arranged the sign on the couch along
with the necklace and pillow.
She waited and waited.
Finally, just when Grandma was asking her if
she wanted a grilled cheese sandwich for lunch,
the phone rang.

"Hello," said Grandma. "Yes. Oh my! That's wonderful news! Congratulations!"

When Grandma hung up, she told Hannah and Sam, "Your mama had a healthy baby boy! His name is Benjamin."

"Hooray!" yelled Sam. He started to dance.

"Are you sure it was a boy?" said Hannah. "It can't be a boy!"

Hannah grabbed the poster, the pillow, and the necklace off the couch and went to sit under the kitchen table.

"Hannah, don't you want any lunch?" asked Grandma.
"NO!" said Hannah. "I want a sister!"

"A baby brother is nice," said Grandma.
"No, it's not! A baby brother is terrible. I hate baby
    brothers!" said Hannah. "How could they do this to me!"

Hannah stayed under the table all afternoon.
Finally she got hungry, so she came up for dinner.
Then Grandma said, "Let's go to the hospital and
see this new baby brother of yours."

They met Daddy in the lobby of the hospital.

"Wait till you see your new brother," he said to Hannah and Sam. "He's the biggest baby in the nursery!"

They rode the elevator to the fourth floor. They looked through the window of the nursery.

There were tiny babies in bassinets lined up in rows.

Some babies wore pink caps, some babies wore blue.

"There he is!" said Daddy, pointing to a baby in a blue cap in the front row.

Daddy was smiling. Grandma was hugging Daddy.

Sam was jumping up and down to get a better view.

Hannah was looking at a sweet baby in a pink cap.

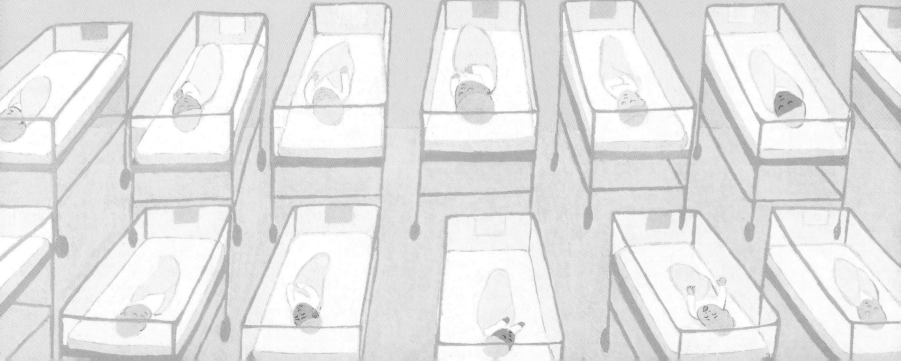

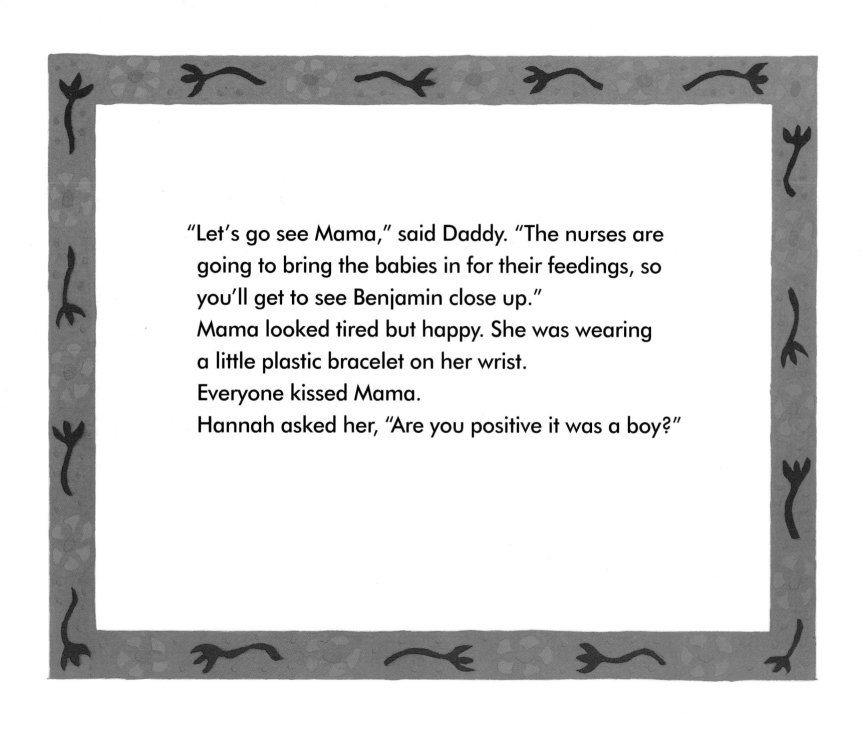

"Let's go see Mama," said Daddy. "The nurses are going to bring the babies in for their feedings, so you'll get to see Benjamin close up."

Mama looked tired but happy. She was wearing a little plastic bracelet on her wrist.

Everyone kissed Mama.

Hannah asked her, "Are you positive it was a boy?"

The nurse wheeled in a bassinet with a baby in a blue cap.

"Here's your baby Benjamin!" she said as she placed him in Mama's arms.

After Mama fed him and burped him and kissed him, she asked Hannah if she'd like to hold him. Hannah sat with Grandma on the chair next to Mama's bed. Daddy placed the baby in Hannah's arms.

Grandma helped Hannah. "Be careful of his head," said Grandma.

Hannah looked at the baby's tiny nose and tiny mouth.

She looked at his round pink cheeks and tight little fists.

When she put her face close to his, she could feel his puffs of warm air and smell his baby smell.

"Hannah, you are going to be such a wonderful big sister. Look how happy he is, sleeping in your arms!" said Mama.

Hannah looked at Benjamin. Maybe he would love fudge swirl ice cream. Maybe she could wheel him around in the stroller. Maybe "Hannah" would be his first word.

"What do you think, Hannah?" asked Grandma.
"I think he's pretty cute for a baby brother," said Hannah.
Sam said, "It's my turn to hold him. Give him to me!"

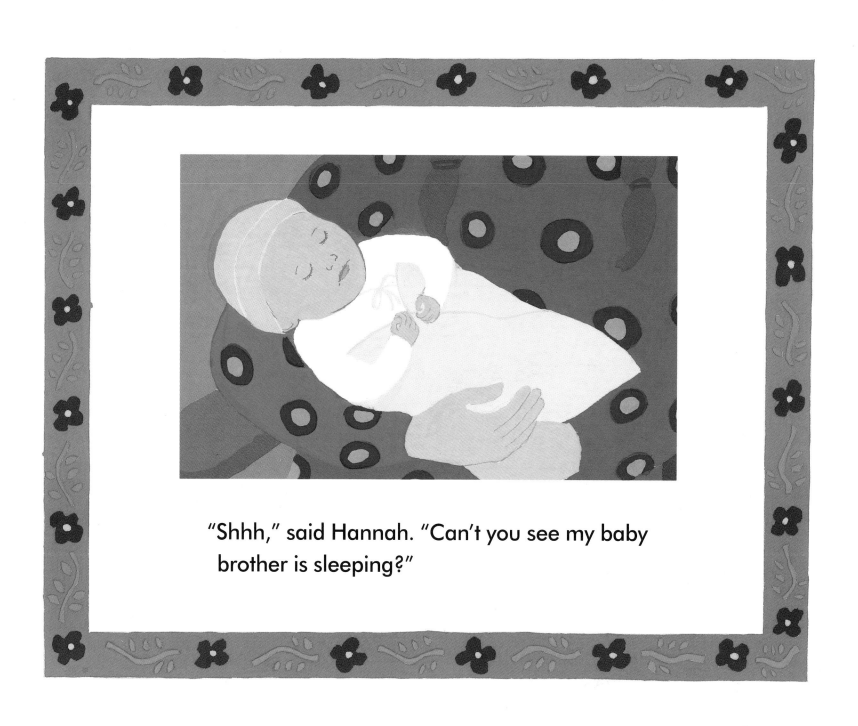

"Shhh," said Hannah. "Can't you see my baby
brother is sleeping?"